This Topsy and Tim

book belongs to

A catalogue record for this book is available from the British Library

This title was previously published as part of the *Topsy and Tim Learnabout* series
Published by Ladybird Books Ltd
80 Strand London WC2R ORL
A Penguin Company

11

© Jean and Gareth Adamson MCMXCV
This edition MMIII

ISBN-13: 978-1-90435-123-8

Printed in China

Topsy+Tim

Look After
Their Pets

Jean and Gareth Adamson

Topsy and Tim's smallest pet was
Tubby mouse. Tubby was really Tim's
mouse but Topsy played with him too.

Every evening, after school, Tim put
a teaspoonful of crushed oats and
sunflower seeds into Tubby's dish.
Sometimes he gave Tubby treats,
like a piece of bread soaked in milk
or water, or bits of carrot or apple.
Tubby liked his treats.

Tubby liked to play outside his
cage. Twice a week, Mummy
helped Tim to clean out the cage,
while Topsy kept an eye on Tubby.
Mummy washed the cage clean.
Tim spread new sawdust on the
floor and put fresh hay in
Tubby's sleeping box.

"I'll fill Tubby's water bottle,"
said Topsy one evening.
"No," said Tim. "He's my
mouse, so I fill his water bottle."
Topsy cupped her hands and
gently scooped Tubby up.
"I wish I had a mouse," she said.

"We don't want another mouse," said Mummy. "They might have lots of babies and we wouldn't be able to look after them properly."
"I'd look after them," said Topsy.
"No," said Mummy and that was that.

Topsy went to feed the goldfish, Sam and Roundabout. Topsy liked them, but they weren't as much fun as a mouse.

Sam and Roundabout lived in a
proper, rectangular fish tank. It stood
in a shady corner of the room. Dad
had fixed some water weed to small
rocks with elastic bands. Sam and
Roundabout liked to nibble the weed.

"Mummy," said Topsy, "the fish
need more water."
Mummy floated a piece of
clean paper on the water.

She gave Topsy a jug of fresh water to pour gently on to the paper. "That stops the tank getting stirred up," she said.

Topsy filled the tank very
carefully. Then she
took the paper
out. Sam and
Roundabout
swam happily in
their clean water.

Topsy gave them a little pinch of
fish food. She knew she mustn't
overfeed them.
"Don't forget to put the cover back
on the tank," said Mummy.
"We don't want Kitty to put her
paw in and catch them."

Topsy and Tim went into the garden to look after Wiggles, their black and white rabbit.

"I'll put Wiggles in his run. Then we can clean his cage," said Tim.

"You mustn't pick him up by his ears," said Topsy.

"I know that!" said Tim. Tim lifted Wiggles out of his cage very carefully, keeping one hand underneath, and put him safely in his run. Topsy cleaned out the hutch and put in fresh straw.

Topsy filled Wiggles' dish with oats and bran and put clean water in his drinking bowl. Mummy gave Tim some apple, carrots and lettuce leaves to put in Wiggles' run.

While Topsy and Tim were playing with Wiggles, Josie Miller came to see them. She was carrying her hamster cage. "Please will you look after Lily for me?" she said. "I'm going away on holiday for a week."

Topsy and Tim ran to ask
Mummy if they could.
"All right," said Mummy, "but
Josie must tell you how to look
after a hamster."

Josie gave them a packet of hamster food. "You must fill Lily's dish every evening," she said.
"She also likes bits of apple, carrot, lettuce or cabbage, and she loves nuts!"

Just then, Lily popped out of her
nest box and went to her food dish.
"Isn't she eating a lot!"
"She isn't eating it," said Josie.
"She's filling the pouches in her
cheeks. Then she will put the food
in her food store to eat later."

Josie asked Topsy and Tim to clean
out Lily's food store every other day,
so that it didn't get smelly. "And
please will you fill her water bottle
every day," said Josie.
"I'll do that!" said Topsy.

"She's got an exercise wheel like Tubby's," said Tim.
"Yes," said Josie. "You'll hear her playing in it at night-time."
Just then, Tubby climbed into his wheel and had a spin.

"Lily will have a lovely time with Topsy
and Tim and their pets," said Mummy.
"Goodbye, Lily," said Josie. "Have a
good holiday with Topsy and Tim!"